Artlist Coll... W9-AAL-732
THE DOG™

Water Dog Hero

By Howie Dewin
photography by Victor A. Coreas

SCHOLASTIC INC.

New York	Toronto	London	Auckland
Sydney	Mexico City	New Delhi	Hong Kong

For
Arenal

ISBN 978-0-545-21212-0

© 2010 artlist

photography by Victor A. Coreas

Published by Scholastic Inc. All rights reserved.
SCHOLASTIC and associated logos are trademarks and/or registered trademarks of Scholastic Inc.

12 11 10 9 8 7 6 5 4 3 2 1   10 11 12 13 14/0
Designed by Deena Fleming
Printed in the U.S.A.   40
First printing, February 2010

Meet Barlow

Barlow is a Portuguese Water Dog (also called a "Portie"). He was born in a fancy kennel with other Porties. But Barlow knew that something about him was different. His favorite thing was to run and play. The other Porties *loved* the water. Barlow was scared of it. Barlow's owner took him to a shelter for unwanted dogs. "He's a Portuguese Water Dog," the owner told the shelter worker, "but something's wrong with him. Good luck finding anyone who would want him!"

Chapter 1

"Look at this one!" said a boy as he walked past the caged dogs at the Bay City Animal Shelter.

The boy rushed past two of the cages. The dogs inside barked as he ran by. The boy knelt down in front of the last kennel. A dog with black curly hair and white paws sat inside. When the boy put his hand near the cage, the dog reached out and licked it.

"Hi!" the dog barked. He wagged his tail hopefully.

"He's a beauty, Andy," his father said.

"He looks just like the dogs at the ballpark, Dad!" Andy said. "Can we get him? I've always wanted to have one of the Bay City Ball Dogs!"

"Say yes!" Barlow barked at Andy's dad. "Please!"

Then Barlow went quiet. He did everything he could to look perfect.

Barlow couldn't believe this was happening. He thought he would never be adopted. Not after what had happened with his first owner.

"You like Barlow?" Eve asked. She ran the shelter. "He's a purebred Portuguese Water Dog! They're nice dogs." Eve opened Barlow's

cage door and let Andy wrap his arms around Barlow.

Barlow leaned into the boy. It felt good to be hugged. He missed the warmth of being near his mom and his brothers and sisters. Barlow's whole family had stayed behind when he was taken to the shelter. None of them had Barlow's problem with water. They were all perfect Portuguese Water Dogs. Not like Barlow.

"I think he likes you as much as you like him, Andy!" his dad said.

"He's perfect!" Andy announced. "He is *my* dog, Dad!"

"Let's fill out the paperwork," Dad said to Eve. "It looks like Andy has found his match!"

Barlow wagged his tail. Could it be true? He thought he had to live in this shelter forever.

"Come on, boy!" Andy called. "Let's go home!"

It is true, Barlow thought. *I'm going to have a home!*

★ ★ ★ ★ ★ ★

"Don't you think he's great, Dad?" Andy said

from the backseat as they drove home. "Don't you think he looks just like the dogs down at the ball field? Do you think they'll let Barlow be a Bay City Ball Dog? Do you think he'll be good at it? Do you—"

"Andy!" said his dad. "I can answer only one question at a time!"

Andy laughed and wrapped his arms tighter around Barlow.

"I guess I have to calm down," Andy agreed. "I don't want to make Barlow nervous on his first day home. We have plenty of time to head down to the ball field and watch the Ball Dogs." Andy turned to Barlow and said, "Wait till you see them, Barlow! We have our own minor league baseball team, the Bay City Sluggers! And they have dogs on the team who retrieve the home runs! Just wait! You're going to love the dogs on the team!"

"I love fetching sticks!" Barlow yipped, even though he knew Andy couldn't understand what he was saying. "And chewing on them!"

"Sounds like he's ready," Dad said. He

smiled at Andy in the rearview mirror as they pulled into their driveway.

"Here we are, Barlow," Andy whispered. "Welcome home."

Barlow stared out the window. It was a beautiful house. The yard was big and green. Barlow imagined playing with Andy.

"Come on!" Andy said as he led Barlow out of the car.

Just then, sprinklers came on across the lawn. Barlow froze.

"Don't be scared," Andy said. "That's just Sheba, our cat."

Barlow was confused. What was Andy talking about? Then he realized that Andy was looking at a cat that Barlow hadn't even noticed.

"She's nice, Barlow," Andy said. "I promise."

"Okay," Barlow yipped. But he was worried about the sprinklers, not the cat.

"Sheba? Say hello to Barlow. He's a Portuguese Water Dog! You're going to be great

Dogs and Water

Most dogs like water, if they're given the chance. But there are some dog breeds known for their love of water. Labradors, Poodles, Newfoundlands, Portuguese Water Dogs, and Brittany Spaniels are some of the most water-friendly dogs. But in all these breeds, there are always individual dogs who don't like to swim.

friends." Andy headed toward the front door.

Barlow turned back to Sheba. The cat was eyeing him strangely.

"*Water* dog?" Sheba laughed. "So how come the sprinkler's got you on the verge of a nervous breakdown?"

Barlow's heart raced.

Oh, no! Barlow thought. *Sheba knows my secret! She knows I'm terrified of water! What if*

Andy finds out? What if he doesn't want a Portie who can't swim? Will he send me back to the shelter?

"What are you?" Sheba giggled. "A cat?"

"Please," Barlow whimpered. "Don't tell anyone!"

Porties were used to herd fish into nets by Portuguese fishermen. In Portugal, they are called Cao de Agua.

Chapter 2

The next day, Andy couldn't wait to take Barlow to the ballpark.

"It's a perfect day!" Andy said to his dad.

"Why's that?" his dad asked.

"It's Saturday. I've got Barlow. And we're heading down to the ballpark to watch Joe Segalla hit practice balls for the Bay City Ball Dogs!"

"You're right, Andy," his dad agreed.

"Come on, Barlow!" Andy clipped on Barlow's leash. The boy and his dog headed out the door. They ran together for several blocks.

Perfect day! Barlow agreed.

Just then, they turned a corner. A round building stood before them.

"That's it, Barlow!" Andy shouted. "That's the stadium! Isn't it cool? Let's go sit behind

I love being with Andy.

home plate and watch Joe Segalla. Then we'll go watch the dogs!"

"Whatever you want!" Barlow barked.

Andy ran through the corridors of the empty stadium. He knew exactly where to go.

Andy suddenly stopped. "Look at that, Barlow!" the boy whispered.

Barlow turned a corner and a big green field stretched out before him.

"Wow!" Barlow barked.

Andy and Barlow ran down dozens of steps until they were right behind home plate.

"That's Joe Segalla," Andy whispered to Barlow. "He's the best player on the team. I wouldn't be surprised if he gets called up to the majors next year."

CRACK!

The ball sailed off Joe Segalla's bat. It soared over the outfield fence. Barlow stood up and pulled on the leash. He wanted to fetch the ball.

"That's right!" Andy laughed. "That's just what the Bay City Ball Dogs do! They retrieve the home runs! Let's go watch them!"

They took off. Barlow loved running. But running alongside his own boy was better than his best dream.

They ran outside the stadium walls. Barlow knew this was where the home-run ball had fallen.

"It's around here, Barlow," Andy shouted. "This is where all the home-run balls land!"

"Can't wait!" Barlow barked.

"And that," Andy said, "is where the Bay City Ball Dogs retrieve them!"

Barlow came to a halt. He tried to understand what Andy meant.

"The dogs are out *there,*" Andy said. He pointed to a little boat floating on a big body of water.

A small whimper escaped from Barlow's mouth. *This isn't happening!* he thought. *Dogs who retrieve baseballs from the water? I can't do that.*

Again they heard the crack of Joe Segalla's bat. Another ball soared over the fence.

Splash! The ball fell into the bay.

"Fish!" shouted someone on the boat. "Go!"

From where they stood, Andy and Barlow saw a dog leap from the boat. It was a big black dog with curly hair.

"He looks just like you!" Andy cried.

Except he's swimming through water, Barlow thought.

"Got it!" the voice called from the boat. "Let's take a break!"

The sound of the engine floated across the water. The boat came toward shore. Now Barlow could make out the figures onboard. There were four dogs, a girl, and a man.

"There they are," Andy said excitedly. "Those are the Bay City Ball Dogs. Can't you just see yourself out there with them?"

Uh . . . Barlow hoped Andy couldn't read his mind.

"That's Mr. Jeffrey on the boat," Andy explained. "He's the trainer. The girl is Ruby, his daughter. Don't mind her, Barlow," Andy said quietly. "She's a little snobby."

The boat slowed as it reached the shore. The dogs leaped off the boat and splashed around in the shallow water.

"Go ahead and introduce yourself, Barlow," Andy said. "They're going to love you!"

"I'll just stay with you," Barlow barked softly. He leaned against Andy's leg.

"Are you shy?" Andy smiled.

"Who is this?" Mr. Jeffrey was walking up to them.

"Since when do *you* have a Portie?" Ruby demanded.

"Since yesterday," Andy said proudly.

"Nice-looking dog," Mr. Jeffrey said.

"Mr. Jeffrey," Andy said nervously. "I've dreamed of having a dog who was a Bay City Ball Dog . . . so I was just wondering if there were any openings. . . ."

"Just because your dog is a PWD," Ruby said, "doesn't mean he can be a Ball Dog. Bay City Ball Dogs are only the *best* of the PWDs."

Andy's eyes narrowed. He never did like Ruby, not since the first time he met her in kindergarten.

"Settle down, Ruby," her father said. "What's your dog's name, son?"

"Barlow," Andy answered.

"And what makes you think Barlow would make a good Ball Dog?" Mr. Jeffrey asked.

"I just think he would. He's a Water Dog, after all. He's smart. And he's a great dog all around," Andy said.

"You know that the Bay City Ball Dogs do important work," Mr. Jeffrey said. "The balls they retrieve get signed by the players. Then we auction them and raise money for homeless animals. We're the only hope a lot of dogs and cats have of finding a home. It's a big job!"

"I know, sir," Andy answered. "I think Barlow would be good at it!"

Barlow's heart was breaking. It was just a matter of time. Somebody would ask him to jump in the water. He would start shaking and be unable to move. He'd start crying. Then Andy would realize that his Portie was not as wonderful as he thought, and Barlow would be sent back to the shelter.

Barlow couldn't listen to the conversation anymore. It was making him a nervous wreck!

"Hey, Jeffrey!" a voice called out.

Andy spun around. Joe Segalla was standing right behind him!

"Ready to get back to it?" Joe asked.

"Sure thing," Ruby answered.

"Who's this?" Joe asked, looking at Barlow.

"This is Barlow," Andy said. He couldn't believe he was talking to the great Joe Segalla.

"And who are you?" Joe asked Andy.

"Andy, sir. It's a pleasure to meet you!"

"Andy was just suggesting that we give Barlow here a tryout," Mr. Jeffrey said to Joe.

"Is that right?" Joe said. He smiled at Andy, then looked at Barlow. "Well, he's got the right look for the job, doesn't he?"

"That he does," Mr. Jeffrey agreed.

"A Bay City Ball Dog has to prove he can get the job done," Ruby snapped. "*My* dogs are not just any dogs!"

"Well," said Joe, "let's give the rookie a chance to prove himself. What do you say?"

"Yes!" Andy shouted.

"All right," agreed Mr. Jeffrey. "We'll do it before the end of the day."

Barlow lay down. He was afraid his legs wouldn't hold him.

Dogs and Sports
Dogs love to run and fetch. But some dogs also participate in "human sports." Have you ever seen a dog play Frisbee? Rollerblade? Surf? Keep an eye out, because some dogs are doing all those sports!

Chapter 3

"Look at that!" Andy exclaimed. He pointed at the dog named Slugger. The big black dog leaped from the boat as the ball landed in the water. "Slugger's the leader of the pack. Did you see how high he jumped?"

"I saw," Barlow barked.

"Slugger is the original Ball Dog, so everyone loves him," Andy continued. "And Fish," he said as he pointed at the next dog. "He's the best swimmer."

"Great," Barlow yipped, feeling worse.

"Diver has the white belly. She's fast! Sometimes she has the ball in her mouth before you even know it's landed! The little one is Squirt. She's the newest member. She's small, but tough!"

Andy hugged Barlow. "I can't wait to see

you out there!" he said.

"Yes, you can," Barlow barked softly. "Believe me, you can."

"I know." Andy laughed. "You're excited for your turn. Don't worry. Mr. Jeffrey promised. You'll be in the water soon!"

Barlow shivered. He had to do something. But what? Should he run away? Should he hide in the stadium? Should he—

"Okay, Andy!" Mr. Jeffrey's voice broke through Barlow's thoughts. "Let's see what Barlow can do."

Barlow's head snapped up. The boat was near the water's edge.

"Bring him down to the water. We'll start with retrieving the ball from the shore."

"You got it, Mr. Jeffrey!" said Andy. "Come on, Barlow! This is your chance!"

Barlow looked from the boat to Andy. His legs wouldn't move, even though Andy was pulling on his leash.

"Come on, Barlow!" Andy said. Slowly Barlow started to move toward the water's edge.

"What's the matter, boy?" Andy asked softly. "You nervous?"

Ruby laughed. Barlow could see Andy's face go red.

"You're a Water Dog, Barlow," Andy whispered. "Why don't you want to go into the water?"

"Never saw a Portuguese Water Dog who

was afraid of water!" Ruby said. "Maybe we'll end up raising money for *him*!"

"Ruby," Mr. Jeffrey scolded. "That's enough!"

"Barlow!" said Andy.

"Don't worry, son," Mr. Jeffrey said. "He might need a little work on the basics before we do a Ball Dog tryout."

Andy looked at Mr. Jeffrey. He saw Ruby silently making faces at him behind her father.

"I don't get it," Andy said softly. "What's wrong with you?"

Barlow's heart broke. He had disappointed Andy, and now everything was going to end.

"That's enough for today!" Mr. Jeffrey announced. "Thanks, everyone!"

You Can Help a Dog Overcome Fear

As soon as you realize a dog is afraid of something, begin working with the dog. First, bring the dog and the feared object together, but not too close. Make the meeting quick and end it with a reward. You may have to repeat this many times. Each time, bring the dog closer to the feared object. Always give a treat or reward. Eventually, the dog will connect the treat with the object and forget about being scared.

The moment was over.

"Come on," Andy said quietly. "Let's go."

The boy turned away from the water, and Barlow followed. The dog's legs moved easily now. He walked right next to Andy and tried to win him back. But Andy's thoughts seemed to be elsewhere.

"Hey, Andy!" a voice called out.

Andy looked up. Joe Segalla was walking toward them.

"Don't worry about it, kid," Joe said. "Not everyone is born to be on the team. Sometimes it takes a while to figure out what your talents

Before the invention of radio, Porties would carry messages from boat to boat in the open sea.

are. You've got a great dog there—even if he may not be a Ball Dog."

Andy tried to smile.

"See you around, kid," Joe said, then headed toward the bay, where the others were wrapping things up.

Andy watched him go, and Barlow could see the disappointment in his eyes. Barlow suddenly realized why this was important to Andy. If Barlow made the team, then Andy would be part of the team, too. Barlow wanted to be able to do that for Andy. But how would he ever be able to overcome his fear?

Barlow didn't have a chance to think about how he might overcome his fear. Suddenly, Andy pulled his leash.

"That's it," Andy announced. "We're going back to the shelter!"

Chapter 4

B arlow had trouble keeping up with Andy. His mind was a blur of frightened thoughts. He saw himself locked up again in the shelter. He tried to think of ways he might win back Andy's affection. But he couldn't stay focused.

"It's this building here," Andy said.

He doesn't seem to care, Barlow thought. *Why isn't he at least sad? Won't he miss me?*

"Come on, Barlow. In here," Andy said matter-of-factly. He pulled the dog through the front doors of the shelter.

Barlow thought he'd never have to face the shelter again. But here were all the old smells — the dogs, the bad food, the disinfectant.

I will never have a home, Barlow thought.

"Excuse me," Andy said.

The woman who had been there when they adopted Barlow turned around.

"Barlow!" Eve said. "And Andy! Right?"

"That's right," Andy said. "Do you have a minute?"

"Sure," Eve said. "What's up?"

Barlow closed his eyes. He waited for Andy to say the words. He waited for him to hand the leash back to Eve.

"Well," Andy began, "I just tried to get 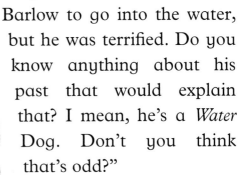 Barlow to go into the water, but he was terrified. Do you know anything about his past that would explain that? I mean, he's a *Water* Dog. Don't you think that's odd?"

Eve laughed. "Well, I did hear something about that," she said. "The breeder who left him here said he wasn't a 'normal' Portie, because he didn't like water. But, personally, I don't put much stock in that kind of thinking."

"What do you mean?" Andy asked.

"Well, I think Barlow is a great dog. He's smart and loving. He just needs a little help. He needs someone to help him get to know the water. I don't care if you are a dog or a person, fear comes from not knowing what you can do if you try. Barlow just needs to realize what he's capable of. Do you think you're the right person to give him that support?"

For the first time since leaving the ballpark, Barlow saw Andy smile. He saw him nod to Eve. The boy looked down at Barlow, but then stopped smiling.

"Oh, no!" Andy said. He kneeled down in front of Barlow.

"What's wrong?" Eve asked.

"Barlow must have thought I was going to leave him here. Look at his face!" Andy put his hands on Barlow's head and looked him in the eyes. "I would never leave you. I just wanted to find out how to *help* you!"

Relief swept through Barlow. He licked Andy's face.

"I love you," he yipped. "I'll do whatever it takes to make it on the team!"

★ ★ ★ ★ ★ ★

The next day, Andy and Barlow went to work. They spent several days getting used to the idea of a single bucket of water. Each day, Andy helped Barlow get a little bit closer. Every time Barlow took a step, Andy rewarded him with a small dog biscuit.

Barlow couldn't believe it. He actually started looking forward to their daily sessions. Nothing was more fun than making Andy happy. And nothing was more satisfying than a treat!

At the end of the week, Andy brought Barlow all the way to the bucket.

"Okay, Barlow," Andy said. "I just want you to put one paw in the bucket. . . ."

Barlow could feel his muscles tighten. He felt his legs start to freeze. But then he saw the look in Andy's eyes—and the treat in Andy's hand! He had to do this!

Barlow lifted his paw and put it in the bucket.

"What a dog!" Andy shouted. He hugged Barlow and gave him the biscuit.

The next day, Andy got the sprinkler out.

"Today I want you to feel what it's like to have water splash on you, Barlow."

"This should be fun!" said Sheba the cat, who was hiding under the car.

"Fun for you, maybe," Barlow muttered.

But Barlow did everything Andy asked. He put his paw in the bucket and stood in the sprinkler. Then he put all four paws in a small pool.

Every evening, Andy and Barlow would go outside and play fetch. Barlow was good at fetching the ball. He just had trouble remembering not to chew it into bits before returning it to Andy.

"That's a tricky one, Barlow," Andy said. "I know how much you love to chew! Don't worry. You'll get it! It just takes practice!"

"I'll get it, Andy," Barlow barked.

"When?" teased Sheba. "Next year?"

Two weeks later, Andy took Barlow down to the creek behind his house.

"This is a big step, Barlow," Andy said. He put his arms around his dog's neck. "I'm proud of you. You've come a long way since the tryout. Now I just want you to stay in the creek and feel the water running past your legs. Once you get used to that, we'll go a little deeper, and you can start kicking your legs. You have webbed feet, you know. You can do this!"

Porties have webbed feet and a rudderlike tail.

"I can do this!" Barlow barked as he stepped in the creek. His heart pounded.

"Way to go, Barlow!" Sheba cheered. "Who's the Water Dog? Oh, yeah! You are! That's right!"

Barlow couldn't help but smile.

"I'm proud of you," Andy said. "Look how far you've come!"

A few days later, Barlow went farther into the creek. Now the water was deep enough for him to kick his legs beneath him.

"I'm paddling in water!" Barlow barked. Joy began to replace his fear. He was swimming! He was finally doing the one thing he never thought possible!

It had been three weeks since Barlow's failed tryout. It was Saturday, and Andy wanted to take Barlow down to the ballpark.

"I wouldn't rush it, Andy," his dad said. "Barlow is making progress, but I think it's smart to work with him some more. Maybe next week would be better."

Andy nodded. He knew his dad was right. But it didn't make waiting any easier. He wanted to show Ruby what his dog could do.

Just then Ruby appeared, walking past his house. "How's your Not-So-Much-of-a-Water-Dog?" she asked.

"He is great!" Andy declared. "Just wait. Barlow is in training and is going to make the team."

Ruby doubled over in fake laughter. "Yeah, right!" she said.

Two days later, the phone rang at Andy's house.

"Hello?" said Andy.

"Andy? This is Mr. Jeffrey."

"Hi!" Andy sputtered. "How are you?"

"Well, I'm in a bind. But you might be able to help."

"How?" Andy asked.

"Ruby tells me you've been working with your dog. She said you told her that he has improved."

"It's true!" Andy said. He felt butterflies in his stomach. "Barlow has been working hard. I'm proud of him."

"Good," said Mr. Jeffrey. "Because Slugger is out with an injury. I'm short a dog, and tomorrow is opening day! Be at the park tomorrow at four P.M.!"

Chapter 5

The next afternoon, Andy and Barlow left the house and headed to the stadium. Barlow hadn't been able to sleep the night before, but tried to hide his worries from Andy.

"I hope you slept more than I did, Barlow," Andy announced. "I was just too excited!"

Barlow studied Andy's eager face as they walked. Barlow wished he could feel as happy as Andy. He wished he was excited about becoming an official Ball Dog on Opening Day. But he wasn't. All the progress that he and Andy had made suddenly seemed like nothing. He didn't feel ready to be a Ball Dog!

"Look, Barlow!" Andy exclaimed as the stadium came into view. "I thought nobody would be here yet, but look at the news vans. You're going to be famous!"

The stadium speakers were already blasting music. People began lining up to fill the stadium seats. Andy headed toward the Ball Dog holding pen. Barlow willed his legs to run.

Get a grip! Barlow thought. *There's no turning back!*

"Look! There he is!" a voice called out. "That must be Barlow, the new Ball Dog!"

Before they knew it, Andy and Barlow were surrounded by people holding cameras and microphones. They were all shouting questions.

"Is this Barlow?"

"What's your name, son?"

"How long have you been training Barlow?"

"How high can he jump?"

Andy couldn't answer one question before another was asked. Barlow could feel his legs getting weaker.

"Give them some space, folks!" Mr. Jeffrey's voice rang out. "Let's not put too much pressure on the new dog, huh?"

Mr. Jeffrey pulled Andy and Barlow away from the cameras. He hurried them into the special area for the Ball Dogs.

"Can we get some pictures?" shouted a reporter.

"Can we see him fetch one for practice?"

"I know Bay City loves its Ball Dogs," Mr. Jeffrey announced to the reporters. "But Barlow is just a beginner. Let's not put too much pressure on him! That's all for now!"

Finally, the reporters backed away. Barlow lay on the ground, trying to catch his breath. Mr. Jeffrey turned to Andy and Barlow.

"Sorry about that, but a new Ball Dog is big news around here. Like it or not, I'm afraid the pressure is on!"

★ ★ ★ ★ ★ ★

A half hour later, Andy and Barlow were following the other Ball Dogs toward the stadium gate. Slugger was in the lead. He limped along with a cast on his front leg.

"How did he hurt his leg?" Andy asked Ruby.

"Bad jump during training. But don't get too comfortable," said Ruby. "Slugger will be better in no time! And then he's back in, and your dog is *out*!"

Andy fell to the rear of the line and walked alongside Barlow.

"Try to enjoy it, Barlow," said Andy.

Barlow looked at Andy. The boy seemed to understand that Barlow was scared. Suddenly, Barlow felt a bit better. Just knowing that Andy understood his feelings helped.

"I'll try!" Barlow barked. He wagged his tail. His heart started to pound. But this time it wasn't from fear. He was excited!

The five dogs reached the gate. They stood in a straight line—Slugger, Fish, Diver, Squirt, and Barlow. They were ready to make their entrance.

"Let's go!" Mr. Jeffrey shouted.

"Walk proud, Ball Dogs!" Ruby called.

The gate swung open and the dogs headed onto the field in a proud row.

"Ladies and gentlemen," called the announcer, "give a big welcome to Slugger. He may be injured, but he's still the team leader of the Bay City Ball Dogs!"

The crowd cheered.

"Fish!" The roar of the crowd swelled for each dog. "Diver! Squirt!"

Finally it was Barlow's turn. To Barlow's surprise, his legs were carrying him along effortlessly. It was almost as if he wanted to be in front of the crowd. He wanted to hear the cheering.

"And now, the newest member of the Bay City Ball Dogs. Please give a warm welcome to Barlow!"

Andy and Barlow stepped through the gate and onto the field. An explosion of cheers and chants rose from the crowd.

"Bar-low! Bar-low!" Barlow trotted and wagged his tail. He barked back at the crowd.

"This is great!" he barked to Andy.

"Look up there, Barlow!" Andy cried. He pointed to the digital screens that loomed over the stadium. On each screen, Andy and Barlow were nearly 30 feet high. "We're famous, Barlow! We're stars!"

Andy laughed and Barlow barked. The boy and the dog were having the time of their lives. Andy's dream of being on the Bay City ball field was coming true. And Barlow knew that he had helped make it happen. It was the best day ever!

Suddenly, the fans went quiet, and music began to play.

"Quiet, Barlow," Andy whispered in his ear. "This is the national anthem."

Barlow sat proudly and listened to the beautiful music. He felt the warm sun.

It's like a dream, he thought.

Then the music ended . . . and so did Barlow's good feelings.

"All right, Ball Dogs!" Ruby called. "To the boat!"

Reality crashed in on Barlow. The moment of glory was over. Now he had to be a Ball Dog. He had to get on the boat and be ready to dive for the balls. His legs began to shake

Gulp!

again. He wanted to hide from the people and the cameras.

"Come on, boy. You're okay! You can do this!" Andy coaxed him along.

By the time they got to the water's edge, it was clear that Barlow was a nervous wreck.

"Don't worry," Mr. Jeffrey said. "Not every dog goes in the water every time. I'll try to keep Barlow on board for this game."

"I thought you said your dog had improved, Andy," Ruby mocked. "I guess you're hoping nobody hits a home run!"

Andy tried to ignore Ruby. He lifted Barlow aboard. He found a seat in the middle of the boat and held Barlow close to him.

"Don't let her get to you, Barlow," Andy whispered in his ear. "She's a bully!"

"She might be a bully," Barlow whimpered. "But she's also right. I *do* hope nobody hits a home run!"

★ ★ ★ ★ ★ ★

By the bottom of the seventh inning, it looked like Barlow's wish might come true. The Bay

City Sluggers were down a run, and nobody had hit a ball over the fence all day. Barlow was beginning to feel relieved. Maybe he would get away with not going into the water today. That would give him a little more time to train. If he just had a little more time—

Crack!

"Segalla got ahold of that one!" Mr. Jeffrey shouted.

"Go, Joe! Go, Joe!" the crowd chanted.

The ball sailed up, up, high into the air.

"It's a homer!" Ruby shouted.

"Get ready, Fish!" cried Mr. Jeffrey. "This is your ball!"

Barlow watched breathlessly as Fish stepped to the edge of the boat and waited to see where the ball would land.

As the ball splashed down, the crowd quickly changed its chant.

"Go, Joe! Go, Joe!" transformed into "Bar-low! Bar-low!"

The crowd grew louder. The stadium screens

showed Barlow's furry face, which looked terrified.

"Bar-low! Bar-low!" the crowd continued to roar.

"It's what the fans want, Andy!" Mr. Jeffrey shouted. "We can't disappoint them! Get your dog over here!"

Barlow's body froze. Andy had to get behind him and push. Slowly, the terrified dog slid across the deck. His eyes were wide. Everything was being captured by the cameras and projected on the stadium screens.

Barlow began to hear a new sound. At first it was hard to identify, but then he knew what it was. The crowd was no longer chanting his name. They were laughing. The laughter grew louder. The more Andy pushed him, the more the crowd laughed. It was so funny—a Water Dog who was afraid of the water!

Barlow crumpled in a heap. He had failed Andy completely!

Andy could hear Barlow crying. The sound

broke Andy's heart. His head filled with questions. Why had he pushed Barlow so hard? Why couldn't Andy just have let him be the dog he was meant to be?

"Stop laughing!" Andy cried. "Stop!"

Andy scrambled toward the middle of the boat. He grabbed a towel and threw it over Barlow's head.

"It's okay, Barlow. I'm sorry. I won't let the cameras take any more pictures of you!" The boy lifted a corner of the towel and covered himself, too.

Do Dogs Feel Emotions?

They sure do. Dogs show their moods through facial expressions, how they move their bodies, and the kinds of sounds they make. Most owners will tell you they know whether their dog is excited, happy, sad, nervous, or frustrated.

Chapter 6

Andy's dad watched the terrible scene from the stands. When the boat returned to the dock, he was waiting in the car for Andy and Barlow. The boy and his dog quickly ducked into the car. They both slid down out of view. The ride home was quiet. When they arrived home, Andy went to his room. Barlow went to his favorite hiding place in the backyard.

When Barlow awoke the next morning, he was still in his hiding place. The night's sleep had not offered any relief. He was still ashamed of his behavior. He hated how much he had disappointed Andy.

"Here you are!" a high-pitched voice exclaimed.

Barlow looked up. Sheba was standing on a thick branch over his head.

"Nice hiding spot! Didn't even know about it myself," she meowed.

"Leave me alone!" Barlow said.

"I'm the least of your problems, my friend." Sheba smiled. "You're on the front page of the newspaper!"

"What?"

"You're famous!"

"Oh, nooo," Barlow whimpered. "What does it say?"

"Not being a reader myself, I can only tell you what I heard the humans saying. Andy's dad read it out loud. According to him, the headline said 'Bar-NO!'"

"Ohhhh," Barlow moaned.

"Then it said, 'Bay City Sluggers hire Portuguese Water Dog who is afraid of water. Let's hope they don't hire any baseball players who are afraid of balls!'"

"What did Andy say?" Barlow whispered.

"Not much," Sheba reported. "He just went back to his room."

Barlow covered his head with his paws.

"Fame isn't easy," Sheba said in a serious tone. "But it's not the end of the world, Barlow."

Barlow looked up. Was Sheba being nice, or was this a trick?

"Seriously," the cat said. "Not every cat knows how to catch mice. But that doesn't make them bad cats. It just makes them bad mousers."

Barlow's heart sank again.

"But I don't want to be a bad mouser," said Barlow. "I want to be the dog that Andy wants me to be. Oh, forget it. He'd be better off if I just disappeared."

"Knock it off! You're acting like a puppy," Sheba said.

"I'm serious!" Barlow said, rising to his feet.

Sheba studied the dog before saying anything more.

"Okay," the cat finally said. "Do what you have to do . . . but if you're really going out there on your own, make sure you keep an eye out for the dogcatcher!"

Why Do Dogs Run Away?
When dogs run away, it's usually because they are pulled by some kind of reward. Or, they believe they are in some kind of danger and need to escape. Roaming is a natural behavior for dogs. But thanks to their ability to create "mental maps," they sometimes know how to find their way home.

Inside the house, Andy's parents were standing in the hall outside his room.

"Andy? Andy, open the door."

His parents knocked on his door. Andy wished they would go away.

"Come on, Andy. You can't hide forever."

Andy opened his door.

"What?" he asked his parents flatly.

"We understand how disappointed you are, Andy," said his mom.

"It was a tough day," his father added, "for both of you."

"But you can't let something like this beat you, Andy," his mom insisted. "And it can't be the reason you give up on your dog."

"Did you love Barlow only because you thought he could be a Ball Dog?" his dad asked. "Or did you love him because Barlow is a great dog?"

Suddenly, Andy felt guilty.

"Have you checked on Barlow?" his mom asked. "How's he doing?"

Andy couldn't take his eyes off the floor.

"I don't know," he finally mumbled.

"It's not right to ask Barlow to be something he's not," his mom said gently. "How would you feel if we decided not to love you because you couldn't play basketball? Or if you didn't get straight A's?"

"You'd never do that!" said Andy.

"Of course not," his mother agreed. "And I know you, Andy. I don't think you would, either."

Andy nodded. "I guess I've been feeling sorry for myself and acting pretty selfish," he said quietly.

Andy went outside. He walked into the backyard expecting to see Barlow. But the yard was empty.

"Barlow!" Andy called. "Come on, Barlow!"

He checked all the usual places, but Barlow wasn't there. Then he started searching every hiding spot he knew. Barlow was nowhere to be found.

"Barlow!" he shouted again. Panic snuck into his voice.

"You find him, Andy?" his dad called from the back door.

"He's not here, Dad!" Andy cried. His eyes were filled with tears. "Barlow is gone!"

Chapter 7

"**A**re you sure?" his mom asked. His parents both rushed into the backyard to join in the search.

"He's not here, Mom," Andy cried. "I've checked every possible spot. He thinks I stopped loving him, and he ran away!"

"Get in the car," his dad said. "We'll search the neighborhood."

"I'll call the neighbors," Mom added. "He wouldn't go far, Andy. We'll find him."

Andy nodded. But in his heart, he knew how much Barlow wanted to please him. "Why didn't I think about Barlow instead of myself?" Andy muttered to himself. His dad backed the car out of the driveway.

★ ★ ★ ★ ★

Watch out for the dogcatcher. . . .

Barlow heard Sheba's warning in his head. He ducked around corners. He ran down alleys. He had no idea where he was going. When his stomach began to growl, he knew it was suppertime. He looked around. He was surrounded by big buildings and pavement.

Barlow had never been in the middle of a city before. He didn't know what to do.

"Psst!"

Barlow spun around.

"Psssst! You! With the curly black hair!"

"Who's there?" Barlow growled quietly.

Be tough! he said to himself. *Don't let anyone see how scared you are!*

"I'm right here! In the alley! Are you blind?"

Follow me.

Barlow focused on the alley in front of him. Suddenly, he saw a tiny dog staring at him. She was so small that she was hiding inside a grocery bag.

"Follow me," the little dog whispered. "And don't be so slow! We don't need the whole world figuring out where we live!"

Barlow looked up and down the street. He didn't know this little dog. But he followed her. At least he wouldn't be alone.

"I'm right behind you," Barlow huffed. He caught up with the little dog in a couple of strides.

"No kidding!" yapped the little dog. "You might want to practice being a little quieter if you're going to live on the streets."

"What do you mean?" Barlow asked.

The little dog stopped running. She looked around to make sure there was no danger nearby. Then she started walking.

"I mean, when you live on the streets, there is danger. It's important to not let everyone know where you are!"

"Okay," Barlow answered. He didn't really want to live on the streets. In fact, he wanted to go home.

"My name is Bitty," the little dog said.

"I'm Barlow," he answered.

"Where did you come from?" Bitty asked.

"Umm . . . " said Barlow. "It's complicated."

"Yeah," agreed Bitty. "I know what you mean. I've been homeless since I was born. Wouldn't it be great to have a real home?"

Barlow couldn't look Bitty in the eye. Suddenly, he felt guilty for having a home. He felt dumb for running away.

"It's nice to meet you, Barlow," Bitty said. She stepped through a broken fence. "You can live with us if you'd like."

Barlow followed Bitty through the fence. A large courtyard opened in front of them. Deserted buildings rose on every side. Everywhere Barlow looked, there were dogs. They were all different shapes, sizes, and colors. They were standing, sitting, and lying down. Old boxes were piled up to make shelters.

"Everyone!" Bitty barked. "This is Barlow. He's new here. Any advice you can give him, I'm sure he'd appreciate."

Barlow tried to say that he couldn't stay. But before he could speak, several dogs came up to greet him. One by one, they said hello. Each dog gave Barlow advice.

"Don't go out during the day," said one dog.

"If you find food, share it. We'll do the same for you," said another.

"Sleep as much as you can," said an old mutt. "You need your strength."

With every bit of advice, Barlow's heart grew heavier.

All these dogs have such hard lives, Barlow thought. *It isn't fair!*

Just then, Bitty trotted up to Barlow.

"Here you go, Barlow," Bitty said. She dropped a chicken carcass in front of Barlow. "It's not much, but it will help you feel better. I'll take you around the neighborhood later. I can show you where to find food for yourself."

"That's really nice of you," Barlow said.

He forced himself to eat the chicken. But it was hard to swallow. He knew he was taking food from Bitty, who really needed it. It made him feel even worse for running away from his wonderful home. It didn't matter that he wasn't a well-known Ball Dog. He had a family and a home. Bitty would do anything to have the life he had.

Why don't they all have homes? Why doesn't someone help them? Barlow wondered.

Suddenly, Barlow remembered Mr. Jeffrey talking about the balls that got retrieved from the water.

"We auction them and raise money for homeless animals. We're the only hope a lot of those dogs and cats have of finding a home."

Barlow looked at Bitty and yipped, "Thank you!" Then he took off toward the street. He was going to make things right!

★ ★ ★ ★ ★ ★

Andy called Eve at the shelter. He hoped she might have a clue that would help them find Barlow. It was getting dark.

"It sounds like you and Barlow have had a tough time," Eve said. "You're right to be putting up signs and doing everything you're doing. But you have to trust how much Porties love their families. If Barlow left because he's upset, he may return. Just because he doesn't like water doesn't mean he doesn't have the heart of a Portie!"

Later that evening, Andy sat on the front

What If a Portuguese Water Dog Was Part of Your Family?
You would have a loyal, smart, and lively companion. But you would not want to leave your Portie alone too much, or in a kennel. Porties like people. They want to be with their families.

step of the house. He thought about what Eve had said.

"The heart of a Portie," he repeated in a quiet voice.

"Andy!" a voice barked.

Andy looked up. Barlow was running toward their house.

"Barlow!" Andy cried.

"We have to get to the stadium!" Barlow barked. "Before the night game starts!"

"I'm so sorry!" Andy cried. He threw his arm around the dog's neck.

"Barlow!" Andy's mom and dad ran out the door.

"He came home!" Andy exclaimed.

But Barlow didn't have time. He had to get to the stadium before the boat took off from the dock. He had to face his fears and dive into the water to catch a ball. He had to do it for Bitty and all the dogs who needed homes!

"You must be starving," said Andy.

"Not now!" Barlow barked. He pulled away from Andy and started running from the house.

"Follow me!" Barlow barked.

"Barlow!" Andy cried. "No, please don't run away again!"

Chapter 8

"I'll get the car!" Andy's dad called.

But Andy couldn't wait. He ran after Barlow faster than he'd ever run. He could barely keep Barlow in sight.

"Come on!" Barlow howled as he ran. "It's important!"

It wasn't long before Andy realized where Barlow was going.

"The stadium?" Andy wondered aloud.

Andy could hear the ballpark's organ music. They were only a block away. The game was about to start.

"Barlow! What are you doing?" he called.

Barlow reached the gates of the stadium, then turned toward the bay. Andy sprinted after him. When Barlow reached the dock, he barked loudly. Ruby and Mr. Jeffrey turned in surprise.

The boat's motor was already churning up the water. The other dogs barked at Barlow from the boat.

"Let me on!" Barlow howled.

Andy finally reached the dock. He tried to catch his breath.

"Go home!" Ruby shouted at both of them. "You had your chance!"

"I'm going to do it this time!" Barlow howled.

The other dogs raised their voices, too. The announcer's voice disappeared in the howls. Andy started to speak. But then he saw the picture that filled the huge screens in the stadium. It was Barlow. Again.

The crowd went silent until they realized who they were seeing. Then they began to chant softly.

"Bar-NO! Bar-NO!" The chant grew louder.

"Barlow!" Andy cried. "Come on, let's go home!"

"I have to help my friends!" Barlow barked. "They need homes. I have to help!"

Fish, Squirt, and the other dogs stopped howling.

"What friends?" Fish barked at Barlow.

"I made a bunch of friends today. They're all homeless. I want to catch a ball. I want to help them get homes."

Fish looked at Diver and Squirt. They seemed to understand. Fish picked up a line in his mouth and began to pull the boat back

Do Dogs Have Different Barks for Different Emotions?

Absolutely! Dog barks say many different things. "Play with me!" or "Stay away!" or "There's danger!" Dogs change pitch, volume, and the length of a bark to make different sounds. Getting to know a dog means learning what his or her barks mean.

to the dock. Diver leaped onto the dock and pulled another line until the boat was back at the dock.

"What's going on?" Mr. Jeffrey shouted.

"I'm going to catch a ball!" Barlow barked. He jumped onto the boat.

The crowd roared as they watched the giant screen.

"It looks like Bar-NO is Bar-GO!" the announcer called.

"Daddy! Make him get off the boat!" Ruby whined.

"No, Ruby!" Mr. Jeffrey snapped. "You coming, Andy?"

Andy jumped on the boat, too.

"Play ball!" the announcer called, and the crowd cheered.

"Hang on, Andy," Mr. Jeffrey called. "The water is rough today!"

Andy sat down quickly. He stared at Barlow. It didn't make sense. The water was choppy. But Barlow didn't seem scared at all. He looked like the bravest dog in the world.

They had reached the middle of the bay when the crowd began to chant again.

"Go, Joe! Go, Joe!"

"It's Segalla at bat!" the announcer cried. "The count is two and one. Here comes the pitch—"

CRACK!

It was an unmistakable sound.

Barlow was the first to look up. The ball appeared high in the air.

"Here it comes!" Mr. Jeffrey shouted. "It's a homer!"

In the 1970s the Portuguese Water Dog breed was almost extinct. There were less than 30 in the world!

Chapter 9

The ball had barely splashed into the water when Barlow leaped from the boat.

"Bar-low! Bar-low!" the crowd chanted.

Andy's eyes were wide. He could barely breathe. He watched Barlow hold his head high in the choppy water.

"Bar-low! Bar-low!" The crowd grew louder.

"*Fish* was supposed to dive!" Ruby howled. Her face was red. "Daddy! Get that dog out of the water!" Ruby stamped her feet.

"Ruby! Sit down!" her father ordered.

But Ruby was too angry to listen. She stomped again. This time, she slipped on the slick surface of the boat.

"Ruby!" her father cried.

Andy turned to Ruby just in time to see her

foot slide off the edge of the boat.

"Help!" Ruby screamed. She disappeared over the edge before anyone could reach her. A wave rose up and swept Ruby under.

Mr. Jeffrey ran to the edge of the boat. He searched the surface for his daughter. There was no sign of her.

"Ruby!" her father shouted.

"Where is she?" Andy shouted.

Barlow turned back toward the boat. Why was everyone shouting?

"Ruby!"

Ruby? Barlow thought. *Why is everyone looking over the edge of the boat?*

A wave crashed down on him. Barlow was pulled under the water. He struggled to the surface. As he did, he saw Ruby just a few feet away from him. The rough water had pulled her far from the boat in no time at all!

"Ruby!" Barlow barked. But Ruby wasn't moving.

Barlow knew he had to get Ruby out of the water—fast. He couldn't help his friends by retrieving balls. He had to save Ruby!

He circled around her until he got his shoulders under Ruby's head. He grabbed her shirt firmly in his mouth and began to swim. It took all his strength to swim through the rough water, but Barlow was strong. He was a Portuguese Water Dog. He was born to do this!

He heard Mr. Jeffrey and Andy shouting at

him. Their voices sounded far away. Barlow kept swimming. He held Ruby's head above water. The shore slowly came closer. He heard the boat coming up behind him. His feet scraped the bottom of the bay.

Just then, Mr. Jeffrey jumped into the water next to him. He grabbed Ruby and raced onto the beach. Barlow pulled himself out of the water. He watched Mr. Jeffrey push on Ruby's chest and blow air into her mouth. Andy

Who's a Good Rescue Dog?
Dogs are trained to rescue people in many different situations. Water Rescue Dogs must be strong and yet not aggressive. That's because people who are drowning often struggle while they are being rescued. Water Rescue Dogs must know how to be firm with the drowning victim without attacking.

appeared at Barlow's side. They were silent.

Ruby lay still on the ground, her eyes shut. Barlow had gotten her to land. But had he saved her in time?

Porties make excellent deaf-assistance dogs, because they can be taught to seek out their masters when specific alarms occur, such as a ringing telephone.

Chapter 10

No one spoke but Mr. Jeffrey.

"Ruby!" he whispered.

Even the crowd held their breath. The entire stadium was still.

Then Ruby coughed. She rolled over and opened her eyes.

The crowd exploded in cheers and applause.

"She's alive!" Andy said in relief. Then he looked at Barlow. "You saved her, boy! You saved her!"

Once again, the cameras turned toward Barlow. His face filled the huge screens of the stadium. But this time it wasn't because people were laughing at him. This time, he was a hero!

Andy felt a big hand on his shoulder. He

looked up and saw Joe Segalla. The baseball hero grabbed Barlow and held him up on his broad shoulders. Then he lifted Andy's arm up in the air. The crowd cheered even louder.

But Barlow knew his job wasn't done. He still had his friends to think about. Maybe he hadn't gotten the ball, but he had gotten everyone's attention. He still needed to rescue his friends! He just had to get all these people to help him! He leaped from Joe Segalla's arms and started running.

"Barlow!" Andy cried. "Barlow, come back!"

"Is that dog crazy?" cried a reporter.

"Follow him!" called another.

A crowd of reporters and fans took off after Barlow. Barlow glanced back as he ran.

It's working! he thought. *Just what I wanted to happen!*

"We're almost there," he howled.

"Are you getting this?" a reporter called to his cameraman.

"I'm rolling!" replied the cameraman.

Barlow arrived at the alley where he first met Bitty. He stopped and turned back to the crowd. He wanted to be sure they saw where he was going.

"He wants us to follow him," Andy shouted.

The crowd filled the alley. They followed Barlow just like Barlow had followed Bitty. Just before he got to the last turn before the open space, he stopped. The crowd stopped, too. Barlow stood still. He knew it was important not to scare his new friends. They were street dogs. They were used to being afraid of people. He had to be sure the people understood they needed to be kind and gentle.

"Bitty? Everybody?" Barlow barked quietly. "Don't be afraid. I've brought help."

"What's he doing?" someone whispered to Andy.

"I'm not sure," Andy said softly. "But I think we're supposed to be quiet."

Just then, Bitty appeared.

"Barlow?" she answered, and then froze. "What did you do?" she whispered to Barlow. "You told everyone where we hide?"

"They're here to help, Bitty," Barlow said. "Please trust me!"

Barlow turned and led the crowd around the corner. The homeless dogs froze in fear. Barlow turned to Andy and whimpered quietly.

"These are your friends?" Andy asked.

What have you done?

"Yes!" Barlow barked.

"And you want to help them?" he said.

"Yes!" Barlow barked. He jumped up on Andy and licked his face.

Suddenly, bulbs were flashing. Reporters were talking. The people who had followed Barlow began to look at the different dogs. They knelt down and scratched behind the stray dogs' ears. They reached into their packs and purses for bits of food. One by one, the dogs and the people found their perfect matches.

"Ladies and gentlemen," said a reporter on camera, "we're here with the Bay City Sluggers' biggest hero—Barlow the Water Dog—and he's asking for your help!"

Barlow looked at Bitty, then at Andy. Andy laughed. He knew just what Barlow wanted.

"Do you want to come home with us?" Andy asked Bitty.

Bitty's eyes grew wide with disbelief.

"Say yes!" barked Barlow.

Bitty cocked her head like she didn't understand. But then her tail began to wag. Her ears perked up. "Yes!" she yipped. "Yes!"

Andy laughed and hugged both his dogs. Then he picked up Bitty and held her high.

"Who's your hero?" he asked her.

Bitty licked Andy's face, then jumped down and stood next to Barlow.

"Barlow!" Bitty barked. "Barlow the Water Dog!"

"Yes," said Andy. "He's my hero, too."